ALIENS

THE BEACH BUOY

Collect all the books in the *GUNK Aliens* series!

JONNY MOON

GUNK ALIENS

THE BEACH BUOY

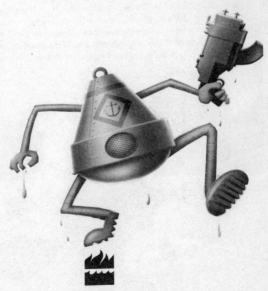

HarperCollins *Children's Books*

First published in paperback in Great Britain by
HarperCollins *Children's Books* 2010
HarperCollins *Children's Books* is a division of HarperCollins*Publishers* Ltd
77-85 Fulham Palace Road, Hammersmith, London W6 8JB

The HarperCollins website address is:

www.harpercollins.co.uk

1

Copyright © HarperCollins 2010
Illustrations by Vincent Vigla
Illustrations © HarperCollins 2010

ISBN: 978-0-00-732616-7

Printed and bound in England by Clays Ltd, St Ives plc

Special thanks to Colin Brake,
GUNGE agent extraordinaire.

A long time ago, in a galaxy far, far away, a bunch of slimy aliens discovered the secret to clean, renewable energy...

... snot!

(Well, OK, clean-*ish*.)

There was just one problem. The best snot came from only one kind of creature.

Humans.

And humans were very rare. Within a few years, the aliens had used up all the best snot in their solar system.

That was when the Galactic Union of Nasty Killer Aliens (GUNK) was born. Its mission: to find human life and drain its snot. Rockets were sent to the four corners of the universe, each carrying representatives from the major alien races. Three of those rockets were never heard from again. But one of them landed on a planet quite simply *full* of humans.

This one.

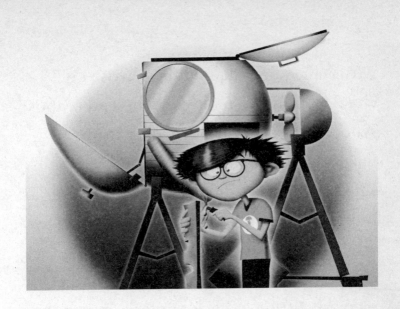

cHAPTER ONE

Jack Brady whistled happily as he worked.

Well, it was a sort of whistle.

Actually, to be totally honest, Jack had
never really got the hang of whistling. He
made up for it by sucking air over his teeth
and humming at the same time, which was
a long way short of actual whistling, but
made Jack feel happy.

It was a hot August day, the sun

was shining brightly and there wasn't a cloud to be seen in the sky. The end of the school term already seemed a distant memory, but there were still weeks of summer holidays stretching out into the future, keeping the prospect of returning to school at a comfortable distance. Most children were enjoying the great weather, playing outside in back gardens and on the streets, firing super-soakers at each other, splashing in paddling pools, kicking footballs around.

Jack Brady, however, was not doing any of these things. Jack was not like most children of his age. Jack was a genius. Jack was an inventor. And right now, Jack was in one of his favourite places – the tree house he shared with his best friend Oscar – fiddling with his latest project. It was an inflatable submarine that he had been toying with for some time and, using a few beach lilos, he was finally making a working prototype. Fixing the various inflated sections together with waterproof superglue (which he had also invented) was a difficult procedure and Jack had to take great care. Very patiently, he applied a thin coating of his adhesive to a section of the sub and set the next piece in place over the sticky trail.

Suddenly there was a noise like a hailstorm as something hit the window of the tree house. Startled, Jack hurried across to the door and pulled it open. As he stepped out on to the porch area he was hit in the face by a handful of stale breadcrumbs.

"Sorry!" came a voice from below. It was Oscar, standing beneath the tree. In Oscar's

hand was a plastic bread bag.

"What are you doing?" demanded Jack as he hurried down the steps fixed to the tree trunk.

"Mum gave me some breadcrumbs to feed to the ducks," Oscar began to explain.

"I'm not a duck!" complained Jack, reaching the ground.

"It's OK – there's plenty left," said Oscar, missing the point as usual. If Jack was a genius (and he was) Oscar was special in other ways. According to Jack's mum, Oscar was a sandwich short of a picnic, and even Jack had to admit that Oscar could be mind-bogglingly stupid at times – but he was loyal and brave and, no matter what, he was Jack's best friend.

"Snivel," Jack called. "Walkies."

In response a unique-looking dog appeared at his feet. Snivel was a mess of legs and hair that defied identification as any particular breed. Some people thought he was some kind of crossbreed terrier, some people thought he had some poodle in him and others just called him a mutt.

None of those people was right. In reality, Snivel was an artificial creature. A Snot-Bot, to be precise. Built using alien technology, Snivel had been given to Jack to help him locate and capture some dangerous aliens that were at large in his area. That mission had been accomplished now, leaving Jack with nothing but a slightly odd three-eyed dog, and the memories of some great adventures.

Jack, Oscar and Snivel headed to the park. One way or another, a lot of their escapades had started here, and for a while it had become a place of excitement and mystery. Now, weeks since their last unusual adventure, it had begun to lose all those associations. Now it was just the park again, a normal place where normal things happened.

Jack looked round as they walked through the gate and sighed.

"Everything looks normal," he muttered with a slightly heavy heart.

Oscar nodded. "Yep," he agreed in a bored tone. "Normal kids playing normal football, normal mums pushing normal buggies, normal dogs taking their owners for normal walks..."

"And Ruby," added Jack in the same tone, "dressed as a Brownie and collecting litter..."

His voice trailed off as he realised what he was saying. Jack and Oscar exchanged looks.

"*Brownie* uniform?" repeated Oscar.

"*Litter?*" replied Jack.

In unison they shook their heads and rubbed their eyes before taking another look. No, they had been right the first time. There was Ruby in a pristine Brownie uniform, holding a black bin liner in one hand and a grabbing stick in the other, with which she was patiently picking up litter. Jack and Oscar hurried over to join her.

As she saw them coming, Ruby turned a bright shade of pink. "Don't say a thing," she told them, but they couldn't stop themselves.

"Litter?" asked Jack.

"Brownie uniform?" said Oscar at the same time.

Ruby sighed.

"It's a long story," she said them.

Ruby was the final member of their team. When Jack had been recruited by the mysterious Bob to be a member of GUNGE (the General Under-Committee for the Neutralisation of Gruesome Extraterrestrials), he had quickly realised that he needed more than just a three-eyed robotic dog to help him. Naturally he had turned to his best friend Oscar.

Then both he and Oscar had met Ruby.

At first, Jack and Oscar had worried about having a girl in the team. But Ruby had become an invaluable companion in all of Jack's missions to capture the evil GUNK aliens. She shared Oscar's love of adventure and danger, but with the dial turned up to maximum. Ruby was a complete adrenaline addict with a passion for dangerous sports and activities. The only problem was that her mother was very protective and insisted that Ruby spend her time on safer pursuits, like ballet and flower arranging. To maintain her sanity, Ruby spent a lot of her time *pretending* to do the things her mother wanted her to do while really following her own agenda – which meant that she was often to be seen surfing in a ballerina's tutu, or rock climbing in jodhpurs.

"Mum wanted me to join a club," Ruby explained, "so I suggested the Brownies."

Oscar and Jack just shook their heads, not getting it.

"Thing is, after the Brownies, you can join the Guides or the Scouts," Ruby continued, "and then you get to go on camps and rock climb, and abseil and paraglide, and all sorts of things…"

"So this is a long-term plan?" asked Jack, beginning to understand her thinking.

"Brilliant, isn't it?" said Ruby. "For once I'm doing exactly what Mum wants, but eventually it'll lead to exactly what *I* want. It's a win-win scenario."

"Except for having to wear that uniform," pointed out Oscar.

"Well, yes, of course," Ruby confessed.

"And collecting litter," said Jack.

Ruby sighed again. "I have to get my community service badge before I can do anything exciting. But let's face it, it's not as if there's anything else going on, is there?"

She looked both of them in the eyes, but both boys quickly looked away. Over the last few weeks there had been an unspoken agreement between them not to talk about their adventures with GUNGE. Ruby was on the verge of breaking that understanding and neither Jack nor Oscar really wanted to talk about it.

"Well, it's true, isn't it?" persisted Ruby bluntly. "I take it there's been no word from GUNGE?"

Jack had to agree that there hadn't been contact of any kind.

Ruby shrugged. "So there you are then – it's over."

Suddenly Snivel barked loudly. The three children turned to look at the robot dog. Snivel was staring up into the branches of a tree and jumping up and down – or trying to anyway. With his three eyes he tended to be pretty clumsy.

"What is it?" asked Jack. He looked up where Snivel was looking. There on a branch was a grey squirrel. The squirrel was unnaturally still, and didn't even appear to be breathing. For a long moment the five of them looked at each other without blinking – the three children, the robot dog on the ground and the squirrel up above them – then, finally, the squirrel moved. It opened its mouth and spoke.

"Jack Brady – you're needed... by GUNGE!"

CHAPTER TWO

Jack, Oscar and Ruby had become used to some pretty unusual sights and sounds over the course of their alien-hunting adventures, but nevertheless they were shocked by this new development. In the past they had been contacted by GUNGE agent Bob from some odd, not to say downright *implausible,* locations – but this time it was different.

"Who are *you*?" demanded Jack.

"Bob," replied the voice.

"But you're a woman!" said Oscar.

"So?"

"Bob isn't a woman," explained Ruby patiently.

"Could be," said the voice, slightly defensively.

"But Bob's a bloke," insisted Jack.

"The last one was," agreed the voice emerging from the squirrel. "But I'm the new Bob. And I'm not."

"Not what?" asked Oscar, now thoroughly confused.

"Not a bloke," said the voice, rather testily now.

"So you're the new Bob," said Jack carefully.

"Exactly," said Bob. "Better than the last one."

"You mean you're not a double agent for

evil aliens intent on invading Earth and making us all snot slaves," said Jack pointedly.

"Well, yes, there were some loyalty issues with the last Bob," agreed the new Bob, slightly defensively.

"Some loyalty issues!" exclaimed Ruby in shock. "He only sold out the entire planet to the GUNK Aliens. He used the Blower to contact the alliance and alert them to our existence!"

"Exactly – which is why GUNGE needs you. We need a full debrief."

"You're not having my pants," said Oscar hotly.

Jack shook his head. "She means she wants a full account of what happened when we last saw Bob," he explained.

"What's that got to do with my boxers?" asked Oscar.

Ruby sighed. "This might take a long time," she told the squirrel. "Can we go somewhere more comfortable?"

A short while later Ruby and Oscar were sitting round one of the outdoor tables at the park café. Jack joined them, carefully carrying a tray of drinks – three cool lemonades and a coffee.

"Who ordered the coffee?" wondered Oscar as Jack gave out the drinks.

"For our new leader," replied Jack, nodding towards the fourth chair at the table, where a few tufts of artificial hair on top of the squirrel-bot's head could just be seen. "Wouldn't it be

easier to talk face to face?" he added addressing the small robot directly this time.

To the children's amazement the squirrel actually shook its little head, as if it really was New Bob herself. "Operational security," said New Bob tersely. "It is best that you do not see my face."

"Are you really ugly or something then?"

"Oscar!" chorused Jack and Ruby in embarrassment.

Oscar shrugged. "What? I only asked," he insisted.

"It's a matter of safety," explained New Bob, through the squirrel's tiny mouth.

"Yours and mine. Now let's get on with the debrief. I need to know what happened the last time you caught an alien."

The children all began to speak at once and then stopped and tried to take turns. Together they recalled their adventures in the sewers, where they had captured the Slurrisnoat. Bob had used the alien technology at his disposal in the GUNGE headquarters to teleport the three of them and the bulging Snivel Trap directly to him. Bob had then secured the alien in one of the cells and turned his attention to the mysterious Blower device, which the aliens had been intending to use to contact the rest of the GUNK Aliens.

Each of the four aliens that had come to Earth looking for snot (a valuable source of energy for the aliens" technology) had carried with them part of a special communications device which, when connected together, would enable them to relay details of Earth's position to the waiting invasion fleet. With the children's help, Bob had collected all four parts of the Blower. He told the kids that it was a real puzzle trying to work out how to connect the parts and challenged them to have a go. Everyone knew Jack was a genius, even Bob, and he was unable to resist the chance to prove his superiority.

"So Jack fell for it hook, line and sinker," explained Ruby to New Bob. "He actually put the thing together and handed it back to Bob."

Jack flushed red. "Not exactly," he muttered, embarrassed.

"Of course you did," added Oscar, "I saw you. You slotted each bit into the other, made that weird horn thing, and then Bob turned traitor and blew into it. So now the aliens are on their way. Bob – One, Jack – Nil. And it was an own goal too!"

"You actually *constructed* the Blower for Bad Bob?" said New Bob.

"I didn't know he was Bad Bob then, did I?" replied Jack defensively.

"But you knew what the Blower was for!"

Jack nodded. "Of course I did. Which is why I sabotaged it."

Ruby and Oscar looked at him with their mouths hanging open. "Sabotaged!?" they both spluttered.

Jack allowed himself a small grin. "I was suspicious of Bad Bob, but I didn't want him to get angry and hurt any of us either, so I thought it best to play along. I managed to create a short circuit in the power grid when I connected the bits..."

'Brilliant," announced New Bob, clearly relieved. "So the Blower doesn't work?"

Jack shook his head. "Well… yes. It *will* work, but at a reduced power level."

There was silence for a moment.

"Oh, well, that's better than nothing I suppose," said New Bob, eventually.

"Also, in all the confusion as we left the base, I managed to use another piece of alien tech that Bob had lying around to generate an interference wave that should cancel out the signal," added Jack. "I reckon the Blower signal will have been active for no more than five minutes."

"Long enough to get a message through to the GUNK Aliens," mused New Bob.

"But perhaps not long enough for them to get a solid fix on our location," suggested Jack.

"You mentioned confusion," said New Bob. "How exactly *did* you escape?"

"Team effort," answered Oscar, proudly.

Ruby picked up the story. "As soon as Bob used the Blower we knew he was a baddy. So we sort of… bundled him. Snivel started it – he bit his leg."

"Bob dropped the Blower and grabbed his leg," added Oscar.

"Making him rather off balance," continued Jack. "So when we rushed him…"

"We knocked him to the ground," Ruby said. "And when he fell, his remote control thing dropped out of his pocket and I picked it up."

The children explained that they had run off down the corridor and used the remote control to first open a door and then lock it behind them. They found themselves in a storeroom full of alien technology.

"Including a sub-space instant communicator which I used to set up the interference wave signal to block the Blower," explained Jack.

"Meanwhile, we were looking for something to use as a weapon to help us fight our way to safety," said Oscar. "Snivel helped us find a massive stun gun. It was awesome."

"So you were trapped inside the store room," said New Bob. "What happened then?"

"We knew that the base was somewhere in the real world, we just had to find an external door," Jack replied. "Trouble was, by that point Bob had recovered and had released all the aliens to help him."

"Luckily they were still a bit groggy from the sedative that had been keeping them asleep," said Oscar. "So we used the stun gun to put them right back out again."

"We?" said Ruby, looking at Oscar with her eyebrows raised.

Now it was Oscar's face that was red with embarrassment. "OK, *you* used the stun gun," he corrected himself. "I couldn't quite get the hang of it."

The children explained that they had quickly found the external door and had left as fast as they could, hardly daring to look behind them to see if they were being followed.

"But no one came after us," Jack told New Bob. "At first we were on high alert all the time, expecting some kind of attack, but nothing happened. No contact from

GUNGE, no sign of Bob, no alien weirdness... nothing. In a way, we were almost disappointed. When you've been catching aliens in your spare time, normal life becomes kind of... boring."

"Well," said New Bob, "I'm sure we can do something about that."

CHAPTER THREE

The three children sipped their lemonades
while New Bob absorbed their stories.
Behind them the park keeper passed slowly,
picking up litter with a metal pointy stick
and depositing it in a bin bag. He glanced
over at the café and stopped in his tracks.
Were his eyes playing tricks on him? It
looked like a squirrel was sitting at a table
with three kids.

The park keeper took a step closer and his eyes opened wider in horror. It was the *same* three kids he'd had problems with before. The park keeper didn't know what it was about those three, but somehow, whenever they visited his park there was trouble. Should he throw them out? What reason could he give? Perhaps he should just get a little closer and see what they were talking about. Perhaps then he would find an excuse to exclude them. Carefully, he dropped to all fours and began crawling nearer to the café, using the flower beds for cover.

New Bob was reviewing everything that Jack and the others had told her.

"It seems like whatever you managed to do, the Blower signal isn't going to reach the GUNK Aliens for a while, which means you have bought us some time," she concluded. "However there *is* the problem of other aliens."

"*Other* aliens?" asked Oscar.

"Bad Bob told us that there were other alien races in the GUNK Alien alliance, remember," Jack reminded Oscar. "Aliens that didn't get to send representatives on the snot-hunt ships. He said he'd been in direct contact with them. They'll be on their way here to confirm his story."

"Exactly," agreed New Bob. "And we at GUNGE have been monitoring the skies for any sign of alien spaceships ever since. We think one has landed in the last forty-eight hours."

"Well, the first thing they'll want is to see Bad Bob so if we keep watch on his base they'll come to us and we can Snivel Trap "em! Job done!" Jack beamed.

The squirrel jumped up on to the table and stood up on its back legs, waving its arms at the children.

"No, no, no," insisted New Bob. "It's not that straightforward. You see, the thing is, we've lost Bad Bob's base."

"*Lost*?" echoed Oscar.

"How can you lose a whole building?" asked Ruby.

"Easy if your building is full of alien technology," said Jack.

New Bob nodded. "As soon as you left, Bad Bob must have activated his emergency power generator, activated the transdimensional cloaking device for the base, and used the teleport to relocate."

"So the base could be anywhere?"

"No, not anywhere. The range for a
teleport of that mass is limited. The base
must be within thirty kilometres, and he
won't have the energy to make another
jump any time soon. He'll also need

somewhere with plenty of power, so he can recharge the base's batteries and get ready to make another jump."

"So," said Jack, "let me get this straight. We need to find the base, which could be just about anywhere within a thirty-kilometre radius, before the *new* aliens arrive, so we can stop them making contact with Bob and the four aliens we've already captured?"

"Yes," said New Bob.

"So what alien tech can GUNGE let us have to help?" asked Jack.

"Nothing," confessed New Bob sadly, her Squirrel-Bot shrugging its little shoulders in sympathy. "All our alien toys and tech are in the GUNGE base... the one Bad Bob's stolen."

The park keeper fiddled with his hearing aid. Something was definitely wrong with it.

Instead of amplifying sound so he could hear what was going on around him it seemed to be picking up a silly radio play about alien invasions. It must be some kind of interference, he decided. Something to do with all these Wi-Fi hot-spots and mp3 things his nephew was always going on about. Perhaps if he just turned up the hearing aid to maximum...

Suddenly the Squirrel-Bot froze.

"Proximity alert," said New Bob. "Audio surveillance identified. Initiate defence protocol – Snivel Attack Mode Six."

Instantly Snivel got to his feet and started barking loudly. The pitch of his yelps rose quickly until they became inaudible to the naked ear. Not, however, to the sensitive mechanism of the park keeper's hearing aid. With his own scream of agony – much louder that any sound Snivel had made – the park keeper leaped to his feet. And then, slowly, he fell backwards on to his black plastic bin liner of rubbish, unconscious.

"Jolly good," said New Bob. "Right, time to get to work."

As the gang were walking home, Ruby got a call on her phone. She argued for a bit with whoever was on the other end, then hung up.

"Who was that?" asked Jack.

"My mum. She wants me to come home, like, *right now*."

"Really? But we were going to go to the tree house to work out the plan for the mission..."

"Sorry," said Ruby. "I'd better head back. My mum sounded really cross. Actually, she's been really odd for a while."

"Stranger than usual then?" joked Oscar.

Ruby didn't laugh. "Yeah. Really weird. I mean, I know she worries a lot and hates me doing anything that might be remotely dangerous, but she's really taken it to a new level this past month."

"Maybe it's something to do with her job," suggested Jack kindly. "Stress. What is it she does?"

Ruby turned on to the road that led to her house, and Oscar and Jack followed. Ruby shrugged. "I'm never really sure," she admitted. "Something to do with the council. She's always talking about meetings with the refuse committee."

"Maybe she's under pressure to increase recycling," Jack wondered.

Ruby shrugged again. "Whatever it is, she's getting really weird about me going anywhere at the moment, unless she knows exactly where I am. So she's got me tickets for this orchestral concert this afternoon, and apparently I've got to go..."

"Keep an eye out for aliens," Jack suggested. "You never know, the next one might be disguised as a tuba."

Smiling at the idea, Ruby disappeared inside her house and the boys hurried home to start alien hunting.

"So where do we start?" asked Oscar when they were safely up in the tree house.

"Any ideas?" said Jack, looking at Snivel. Snivel shrugged his shoulders, which made his third eye open. He then had to concentrate to close it, causing him to sneeze violently three times and then fall over. He shook his head and got to his feet.

"When we were in the storeroom at Bad Bob's base I downloaded the latest data files on the GUNK Aliens," Snivel told them. "As well as the four lead alien races that we have already encountered, there are fourteen other major aliens in the alliance."

Jack and Oscar nodded. "Fourteen, OK, that's not too bad."

Snivel, however, had not finished. "In addition there are a further sixty-four alien

races who are trading partners of one or more of the eighteen Gunk Aliens races, all of whom use snot-powered technology."

Oscar was using his fingers now to keep up. "Original four, another fourteen, plus sixty-four," he muttered to himself. "Seventy-eight?"

"Eighty-two," Jack corrected him.

"And a further one hundred and eighteen aliens races that live in the same galactic sector as the Alliance, and who might want Earth snot as a tradable commodity," concluded Snivel.

There was a moment of silence.

"So basically, if there was an alien landing in the last forty-eight hours, the alien we are looking for could be any one of about two hundred different alien species?" said Jack, sounding more than a little horrified.

"Give or take," answered Snivel.

Oscar sneezed and absentmindedly wiped his nose on his sleeve. Snivel bounded over to him. "Do you mind?" he asked and, without waiting for an answer, sucked the fresh snot from Oscar's sleeve. "Sorry, but I really needed a snack," he explained. "My power is running low."

"You're in luck," said Oscar, grinning. "I forgot to take my hayfever tablet this morning. Achoo!" He sneezed again.

CHAPTER FOUR

"Are you sure that thing is working properly?" asked Oscar, pointing at the strange-looking device in his friend's hand. It was based on the remote-control that they had taken from Bad Bob's base, but Jack had added components to it, including a tiny model satellite dish that could turn a full three hundred and sixty degrees to indicate direction. As it worked it emitted a stream of electronic burps and bleeps, like an electric cat purring.

"Of course it's working," replied Jack. "Don't my inventions always work?"

Oscar bit his lip and declined to answer. He knew Jack was a genius and wasn't about to argue with him, but his own experience, not to mention the odd scratch and bruise, were testament to the fact that Jack's inventions were not always perfect.

"So tell me what it's doing again?" asked Oscar.

Jack sighed. Explaining things to Oscar could get very boring. "The remote control was the thing Bad Bob was using to operate some of the alien technology in his base. And when I took a close look at it I found that the micro wavelength used for communicating the commands has a certain oscillation pattern that is unique to the alien tech. So I used the remote control to reverse-engineer a tracking device."

"In other words, it's an alien finder," said Oscar.

"Well, strictly speaking, it's an alien energy finder, but yes, that's the idea."

Oscar nodded, finally getting the picture. "So why have we been wandering around in circles for the last hour and a half then?"

Jack shook his head and then tapped the device gently. "I don't know," he confessed. "It's picking up a signal consistently, but I'm not getting any clear directional read out." They had reached a road to cross and Snivel had stopped at the kerb to wait for them. Carefully, they looked both ways then, seeing that the road was clear, they walked across the road, Snivel leading the way as usual. On the other side

Jack consulted the scanner again.

"Still reading the same," he announced. "Apparently somewhere up ahead."

"Again?" muttered Oscar, frowning. An idea half formed in his head. Could it be? No, surely not.

But then again…

"Jack?" he said.

Jack stopped and looked at him.

"Yeah?"

"Could it be Snivel?"

Jack looked at Oscar, then at Snivel, who was a few metres ahead of them along the pavement. Then he looked at the scanning device in his hand, back to Snivel and then back to Oscar again.

Slowly his face turned red. "Oscar, you are a genius," he said, with a sigh.

"I am?"

"And I'm an idiot."

"You are?"

"This is useless as an alien scanner cos it just picks up Snivel. His command systems use the same micro wavelengths." Jack shook his head sadly. He should have remembered that when Snivel was eating Oscar's snot. He was built using alien tech, so of course he'd show up on the scanner Jack had very cleverly built. "We need to go home and think again."

Ruby was not a happy girl. The concert was all right – Ruby liked any kind of music and although classical orchestral music wasn't her favourite, she enjoyed the content of the show. What she *didn't* enjoy was having to spend time with her parents, especially when there was an alien hunt going on. And if the text message she had just received from Oscar was anything to go by, it sounded like they really needed her help. Fancy wandering around with a detector that only detected Snivel!

All through the concert her imagination had been racing with ideas about what kind of alien they might be looking for this time. The concert programme was a collection of "Space" themes and as the *Planet Suite* was being pumped out by the orchestra, Ruby had a brilliant idea. The aliens always gave themselves away by making some silly error and failing to blend in. All she needed to do to find the latest alien was to read the news for something weird!

Carefully, so as not to upset her parents, Ruby pulled her mobile phone from her pocket and opened up the internet browser. Soon she was scrolling through a list of local news headlines. Most of it was really dull: a local MP opening a new school, a famous footballer visiting a youth club, an unusually high number of people with hearing aids reporting a strange and painful sound...

And then she saw it. The headline she'd been looking for! Without meaning to, Ruby let out an exclamation of delight. Her parents shot her a dark look. Ruby glanced up and realised that the orchestra was about to start their next piece and her cry

had disturbed the silence as the conductor prepared to begin.

Ruby mouthed a "sorry", and slipped the phone back into her pocket, aware of her father's eyes watching her. She'd have to give it a moment until he became caught up in the music and then she'd text the boys. She might not be able to be part of the hunt in person, but she could still do her bit.

Jack put the scanner on his workbench and sat back in his chair.

"Shame," he muttered. "That was a really neat bit of kit."

"Never mind," said Oscar, trying to raise his friend's spirits.

"Perhaps I can replace my alien parts with some local components," suggested Snivel, also trying to cheer Jack up.

Jack smiled wearily. "Thanks, guys, I really appreciate you trying to be kind, but it doesn't solve our problem, does it? We need to find a way to locate the alien right now and that," – he pointed at his scanning device – "isn't going to be any help."

Just then a strange noise began to fill the room – the sound of manic laughing. Oscar reacted by jumping to his feet and patting his pockets frantically.

"Is that a mobile phone?" demanded Jack.

Oscar pulled a handset from his pocket. "Yeah, Mum gave me her old one when she upgraded. Trouble is, I can't change this silly ringtone."

Oscar looked at his phone and pressed a few buttons. "It's a text," he told Jack. "From Ruby. She says we should turn on the TV newts."

"Newts?"

"I think her finger slipped. She must mean news."

Oscar got to his feet and began moving towards the door. "Shall we watch it at yours or mine?"

Jack grinned. "No need to go anywhere," he announced proudly, then pulled down a towel that had been hanging on the wall of the shed. Behind the towel was a flat-screen TV.

Oscar's jaw dropped. "You've got TV in here?"

Jack nodded. "I've managed to hook up a wireless connection to the satellite box on the house by boosting the signal through a relay unit so..."

Oscar just looked blank.

"We can get all the channels," Jack translated.

Jack pulled out a remote

control from his pocket and activated the TV. "Let's find the news channel," he said.

Seconds later they had the main news channel on screen. Across the bottom, headlines scrolled from right to left. One headline immediately caught Jack's eye.

"Did you see that?" he asked.

"All those deaf people getting a nasty shock?" wondered Oscar.

"No, you idiot, the headline after that. The one they're reporting on right now."

Jack turned the sound up.

"...after the jellyfish invasion of recent weeks we now have reports that a shark has been seen in the bay. Today the normally busy beach was all but deserted as locals and tourists alike ask, 'Has Jaws come to Brilcombe-on-Sea?" The town's mayor Richard Scheider insisted today that it was very unlikely that any shark would be found in the cool waters of the local bay and that there was nothing to fear here in Brilcombe."

Jack muted the TV and pointed at the blurry image being shown on screen. It had been taken by an enthusiastic amateur cameraman using his mobile phone, and it showed something dark and mysterious swimming in the sea. The camera work was indeed very shaky, but there was definitely something there, something that shouldn't be.

"That's it," said Jack confidently. "That's our alien." He got to his feet and grinned. "Come on, Oscar. We're going to the seaside."

CHAPTER FIVE

The pretty blonde reporter stood at the end
of the breakwater and waited for her cue.
Behind her, the whole of Brilcombe Bay
stretched out to the horizon, where the first
of a handful of giant sea-based wind
turbines could be seen, looking for all the
world as if they were floating in the ocean.

The journalist's name
was Zana Perkins, although

with her employers her name was mud. For months she had been convinced that she was on the verge of landing the biggest story in the history of news reporting. Zana had seen evidence of alien life with her own eyes – and not just once, but a number of times. Different aliens, all here on planet Earth. The only thing she lacked was proof of her claims. Every time she got close, something would go wrong.

Zana was determined not to give up. The whole thing had become something of an obsession. Her bosses had become worried about her. They'd urged her to take the holiday leave that she'd been building up over the last few years, they'd given her new assignments where her obsession couldn't be exercised, and they'd even tried sending her to cover sporting events. Nothing worked. Zana's obsession was there to stay.

Finally, after the last adventure, where she'd trespassed in the sewers and wrecked a very expensive hovercraft, her employers had run out of patience. Zana had been 'let go'. Which was a polite way of saying she'd been fired. Kicked out. Sacked. Luckily an old friend of hers from her college days had managed to get her a job as a newsreader for a new channel. It was a long way from her previous network job, but at least it *was* a job. The channel didn't even have a presence on satellite or cable – it was an internet only TV channel called NetNews.

Zana sighed, waiting for the crew to get set up. The crew was, in fact, just one spotty kid with a camcorder, a second-hand laptop, a home-made tripod and a pay-as-you-go mobile phone. Zana suspected that he wasn't even getting paid, but was a college kid doing the job for the experience – but she couldn't be sure because the boy, whose name was Kel, hardly said a word to her.

"Ready?" she asked, trying not to sound too impatient.

Kel grunted and gave her a thumbs up sign. He started counting down with his fingers: *five, four, three…*

On *one*, Zana took a deep breath, waited for a beat and then began her intro.

"I'm here at Brilcombe-on-Sea, for a NetNews exclusive Shark Hunt..." Zana trailed off and made a cutting gesture at her neck to tell Kel to stop recording. Further along the bay she'd seen something that had stopped her in her tracks. It was the boys – Jack and Oscar – who she suspected had some sort of involvement with the aliens. If *they* were here, perhaps this story wasn't the waste of time she had expected. A thrill of excitement and anticipation shivered along Zana's spine. This wasn't a Shark Hunt after all, it was an Alien Hunt!

Suddenly a large wave hit the end of the breakwater, and a torrent of cold water splashed all over her. But for once Zana didn't mind the discomfort. She was back in the game!

Oscar and Jack were walking towards the sea, looking out across the bay for any sign of a shark. In the distance they could see the wind farm floating on the horizon. As they walked, the sand went from soft and thin to smooth and hard, the closer they got to the water. A handful of marker buoys were spaced out along the beach.

"Hey, look, free beach balls," said Oscar, happily.

"Not beach balls, beach buoys," Jack corrected gently.

"Beach boys?" replied Oscar, confused as usual. "My dad's got CDs by the Beach Boys."

"Not Beach B – O – Y – S; Beach B – U – O –Y – S. These are marker buoys. At high tide when the sea is all the way in, they float and show where it's safe to swim."

"Oh," said Oscar simply, looking carefully at the half dozen buoys which, he could now see, were stretched out in a straight line, with a similar distance between each.

All apart from one, which seemed to be slightly out of position. But Oscar didn't worry about it for long. He turned his attention back to the sea.

"This has got to be the place," Jack was saying.

"Can you see the shark?" wondered Oscar.

"No, no... but I'm thinking about Bad Bob's base. We're looking for it and the alien is looking for it – and we need to find it first, right? Maybe the shark alien has found the right location but can't pinpoint the base, and that's why it's swimming up and down the beach."

"So how are we going to

find it then?" demanded Oscar.

"By using our brains," explained Jack.
"Well, my brain anyway. What do you see
out there?"

Oscar scanned the horizon. "Er, the sea?"

"And?" prompted Jack.

"Yucky seaweed. It really stinks!"

"Beyond the seaweed."

"A wind farm?"

Jack nodded. "Exactly, and what does a
wind farm do? It generates electricity... And

one thing we know about Bad Bob's base is that it needs a lot of power. I bet the base is hidden out there, somewhere near the wind farm."

The two of them looked out to sea, trying to make out details of the wind turbines. Behind them, one of the marker buoys seemed to move in the breeze. Slowly, almost imperceptibly, the buoy rolled closer to the two boys, as if it was trying to eavesdrop on their conversation...

"I don't think I could swim that far," Oscar confessed.

"You won't have to," said Jack, "What we need is a sub."

"Great idea, I could do with some lunch."

"Not a sub sandwich – a submarine. A vehicle for going under water. And it just so happens I've recently finished making one."

Oscar had a lot of faith in Jack. Jack was, after all, a genius. Nevertheless, even Oscar had second thoughts when he saw the "sub" Jack had made. It seemed more than a little flimsy to him.

It also took them quite a while to get home, load the sub on a trolley, then tow it to the beach using their bikes. It was late afternoon by the time the boys were using Jack's battery-powered pump to inflate the various components of the sub. Luckily, the beach was deserted. Some clever PR person had come up with a story about a gas leak causing hallucinations and people had been warned to keep away. A single policeman had been on duty at the main entrance to the beach, but Oscar had been on holiday to Brilcombe many times and he knew another way, across the sand dunes to the beach.

After what seemed like ages, the sub was finally ready. Oscar and Jack had to wade out through the thick smelly seaweed until the water was deep enough to accommodate the vessel. Carefully, they clambered inside the tiny cabin and sealed the door. The remains of an old tricycle were fixed to the lightweight plastic floor of the submarine, and Jack showed Oscar how to lie flat on his seat and use the pedals to move them forwards.

"It's a bit like a pedalo," explained Jack. "We pedal to generate energy, which drives the fans, which push us through the water. I steer with these controls, which operate two rudders at the back of the craft."

"So what do I do?" said Oscar.

"You pedal," said Jack patiently.

"Oh, OK. Why didn't you just say that?"

Jack sighed.

On the surface of the sea the craft responded well, although the thick layer of seaweed slowed them down a little. Then Jack activated the dive mechanism and the submarine sank slowly under the surface. Luckily the sea was not too deep here. The underwater surface of Brilcombe Bay sloped gently away from the land so the submarine was floating just a metre or so below the surface and a metre or two above the sand below. Visibility was limited, however, and the boys strained to see much around them.

There was something out there though. Lots of somethings.

"What are those things?" asked Oscar, looking out of the animated blobs that seemed to have their sub surrounded.

"Jellyfish," Jack told him. "The news report said there had been an invasion of jellyfish."

"But is it connected?" wondered Oscar, "to the aliens and Bad Bob?"

Jack nodded. "Bad Bob's base uses a lot of energy... that might heat up the sea water and attract the jellyfish. Which means we're on the right track."

Suddenly something large appeared out of the darkness. Something massive and lit by a single glowing light.

"What's that?" screamed Oscar and in his panic he stopped pedalling. The thing was getting closer now and both boys could see a large mouth full of teeth...

Jack was terrified. "I don't know."

Whatever it was, the creature seemed pretty interested in the submarine and head-butted them. The submarine shook.

"Taking evasive action," said Jack, wrestling with the controls.

Suddenly Oscar was aware of something very unpleasant. His bottom and his feet were wet. There was water in the cabin.

"Jack," he called out, his voice trembling, "I think we've got a problem!"

CHAPTER SIX

Jack didn't like water much. He didn't like the deep end at the local swimming pool.

This was much, much worse.

With alarming speed the submarine had just broken apart, the so-called superglue reacting with the water and becoming completely unsticky. Within moments the craft had split asunder.

It was then that things got really unpleasant. The boys had fallen into a mass of squishy, yucky jellyfish so dense that it made suffocation a more likely fate than drowning. Desperately Oscar and Jack waved their arms, trying to make their way through the squelchy, slimy horde. Finally Jack and Oscar managed to grab hold of one inflated section of the sub. Slowly it pulled them through the jellyfish until they broke the surface.

Quickly they took their bearings. They were a long way out to sea, closer to the massive turbines of the wind farm than the beach. They were also surrounded by lots and lots of stinking seaweed. Beneath the surface they could still feel the jellyfish. Oscar shivered as the slimy things brushed against his legs.

"Shark!" he said,
gasping for breath.

"No, jellyfish,"
Jack corrected him.

Oscar just shook
his head and pointed.

Between them and the nearest turbine
the unmistakable fin of a shark knifed
through the water, moving towards them.

"Maybe it won't be able to get through
all this seaweed," said Jack hopefully.

Then, as if on cue, the shark
disappeared beneath the surface.

"Oh, no..." said Oscar.

"Can you see Snivel?" asked Jack urgently.

Oscar looked all around but there was no
sign of the Snot-Bot.

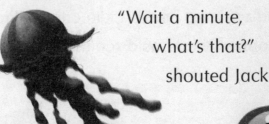

"Wait a minute,
what's that?"
shouted Jack

suddenly. Oscar looked in the direction his friend was pointing. There was a disturbance in the water some distance away – a frantic splashing. Was it the shark? Or the monster that had attacked the sub? There was definitely something dark in the water, fast approaching the nearest of the wind turbines. Now they were closer the boys could see that the turbines were built on small square platforms of concrete jutting out of the sea. At the base of each windmill tower there was a small ridge, wide enough to stand on. As they watched, the splashing thing reached the nearest turbine and something clambered out of the water. The creature shook itself violently, sending a spray of water drops in every direction. When it stopped they could see that it was Snivel – damp but safe.

"We need to get over there," said Jack.

"What's that sound?" asked Oscar. "It sounds like a snake hissing..."

"Or air escaping!" replied Jack. "Our float has sprung a leak."

85

Seconds later it was clear that they were in big trouble. The inflatable was rapidly deflating. The boys began to bob under the seaweed-covered surface, slimy jellyfish all around them.

Suddenly a voice called out to them. "Over here!" A pair of arms reached into the water and pulled Jack clear. He felt himself hauled on to a small rowing boat. Quickly Jack turned and helped his rescuer do the same thing to Oscar. Only when both boys were safely on the boat did he get a good look at the woman who had saved them. It was the blonde reporter they'd encountered on other missions – Zana.

"You!" he exclaimed.

"A thank you might be polite," suggested Zana, seeing the look on the boys, faces.

Oscar and Jack exchanged glances and then both mumbled a thank you. They started removing the clinging seaweed from their bodies, pulling disgusted faces at the texture of the smelly vegetation.

"So where's the alien this time, boys? Is it the shark?" asked Zana.

Neither Oscar nor Jack answered.

"Come on, I know you know that I know all about the aliens. Don't pretend otherwise," she insisted.

A familiar, confused look was materialising on Oscar's face and he struggled to decipher her statement. "What do you know that we know that you know we know?" he wondered.

"You know," said Jack, trying to help. "She knows that we know you-know-what."

Oscar shook his head. "But I don't know what she knows about you-know-what," he spluttered.

"What?" said Zana.

"You know," said Oscar and Jack together.

"No, I don't know," insisted Zana.

Oscar and Jack exchanged a look. "Then we can't really tell you," explained Jack.

Zana sighed. "Look, just tell me what I've got in my net."

Zana shifted on her bench seat to allow the boys to see that at the back of the boat she had managed to capture the shark in a large net.

"It was a bit of a struggle," she confessed. "At first I thought it was going to pull me into the sea, but then it just seemed to go still and I was able to bring it aboard."

Carefully, Jack moved past Zana to take a closer look. He pulled the net back

from the body of the shark. It was covered
with more of the disgusting seaweed.
Gagging, Jack managed to pull the seaweed
off the shark.

"Are you sure it's dead?" asked Oscar.

Jack nodded. "Positive. It was never alive."

Jack picked up the shark body and
moved it back into the middle of the little
rowing boat so Zana and Oscar could see
what he could see.

"It's just a costume," he
said. "A rubber shell.

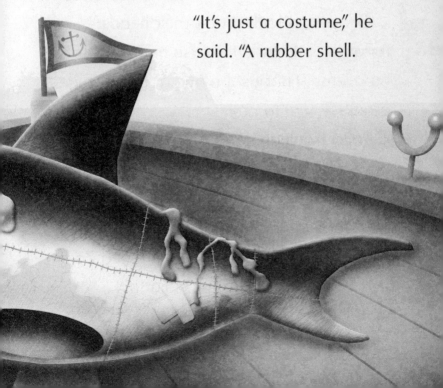

It's got some kind of hole in the bottom."

"Looks sort of head-shaped," commented Oscar.

"You mean you could wear it on your head?" asked Zana.

Jack agreed. "That's what it looks like. You put your head in the hole then swim under water and bingo – instant *Jaws*."

Zana sighed. "So nothing to do with aliens."

Oscar and Jack shook their heads furiously. "Aliens? Of course not. There *are* no aliens. This must be one of those student pranks."

Zana frowned. "Whatever!" She looked across to the closest wind turbine where Snivel was trying and failing to look like a dog barking.

"Why is your dog mooing?" asked Zana.

"He's got a bad throat," said Jack.

"I suppose you want me to pick him up."

"Yes, please," said Jack.

Zana narrowed her eyes. "Well, you'll owe me then. We'll pick up the dog and then you..." she smiled. "Then *you* have to tell me everything you know about aliens."

Oscar and Jack looked at each other again. What choice did they have? Jack met Zana's gaze. "OK," he agreed.

Zana picked up the oars and started to row.

"Where did you get the boat?" wondered Oscar.

Zana smiled. "I drove to the next bay and hired it, then rowed along the sea front."

"It's a nice boat," said Oscar. "I like the heated seats."

Zana stopped rowing and stared at him. "It's a wooden rowing boat," she said.

Oscar shrugged. "So?"

"Wooden rowing boats do not have heated seats," explained Jack.

Oscar frowned. "Then why is my bottom getting so hot?" he demanded. And suddenly he was on his feet. "Ouch!" He wafted a hand at his trousers, which were smoking slightly. Jack and Zana were more interested in the bench seat where he had been sitting. The brown wood was blackening rapidly and dark smoke was beginning to pour from it.

"Something's burning through the boat from below!" screamed Zana.

Even as she spoke the blackened hole burned through completely and water began to rush into the bottom of the boat.

A moment later the boat broke apart and Jack, Oscar and the reporter were deposited into the sea. Jack felt himself sinking into the inky blackness. Suddenly he saw a light in the gloom. He could see that Oscar and Zana had also seen the mysterious glow and were swimming towards it.

But there was something large and dark behind the light.

It was a monster fish. It was huge, with an even huger mouth filled with sharp teeth and a strange tentacle on its head from which the glowing light hung. It reminded Jack of a deep-sea fish that he had once

seen on a TV programme, but this was no
Earth creature. As he got closer, he could
see that the light was artificial. The creature
was a cyborg – part animal, part machine.
An alien cyborg!

The massive jaws stretched open in front of the three humans. Jack grabbed Oscar and Zana by the hand and pulled them upwards. Kicking furiously for the surface they could feel the rush of displaced water as the alien's jaws snapped closed.

Jack broke the surface and saw that they were close to the turbine platform where Snivel was waiting for them.

"Quick, head for the turbine," shouted Jack. When they were close enough Snivel helped them all clamber on to the platform.

The three of them sat down, exhausted by their efforts.

"Now what?" said Oscar, speaking for all of them.

No one answered. They were well and truly stuck.

CHAPTER SEVEN

Zana slammed her mobile phone shut in anger. "It's no good," she complained. "There's no signal."

Jack looked up at the wind turbine towering above them. "No wonder," he said. "With the amount of electrical energy being generated out here there's bound to be some signal interference. I wonder how much energy thirteen of these things generate between them?"

"Twelve," Zana corrected him automatically.

Jack frowned. Had he made a mistake in counting? Oscar began counting the surrounding turbines.

"No, there are thirteen," Jack insisted, confident that he was correct.

Zana shook her head. "I did my research before I came out here. There are twelve turbines in the Brilcombe Bay array."

Oscar concluded his own check. "That's right – I just counted twelve windmills."

"And did you count the one we're on?" asked Jack.

Oscar's face fell. "Oh. Right. That makes thirteen then."

Zana pulled a leaflet from her pocket. It was slightly soggy, but still legible. It was a print out of a press release issued at the time of the wind farm's launch eighteen months ago, and it clearly stated that there were just a dozen turbines in the array.

Jack and Oscar exchanged a look.

"Are you thinking what I'm thinking?" asked Jack.

Oscar nodded. "Someone can't count."

Jack shook his head impatiently. "No – one of these turbines isn't what it appears to be."

"What else could it be?" demanded Zana, butting in to the conversation. "A lighthouse in fancy dress?!"

"BBB," said Jack, to Oscar.

Oscar looked blank.

"Stop stuttering and give me a straight answer," said Zana.

"*BBB*," said Jack to Oscar again, more urgently this time.

Oscar turned to Zana. "I think he's lost it.

Must be the sea water or—"

"Bad Bob's base!" said Jack, losing patience.

"Well, why didn't you just say so?" said Oscar.

Jack sighed.

"Bad Bob's base?" asked Zana. "Is this something to do with the aliens?"

Jack didn't see the point of trying to lie any more. Anyway, Zana had helped them. Quickly and efficiently he gave her a simplified account of the saga of the missing GUNGE base, while she listened with increasing incredulity.

"So a secret organisation that protects the planet from alien invasion has a fantastic HQ which can change size, shape and location, but the organisation was betrayed by a double agent who plans to do a deal with a bunch of aliens who want to enslave humanity in order to farm snot?" said Zana, trying to summarise what Jack had just told her.

"That's about the size of it," nodded Jack.

Zana's eyes widened so far that Oscar feared her eyeballs would fall out of their sockets.

"There's no need to make stuff up," she told him crossly.

Jack shrugged. "You asked for the truth," he reminded her. "But if you can't handle it..."

"So what was that thing in the water?" Zana asked after a long pause. "Was it an alien?"

"Snivel?" Jack called his Snot-Bot over.

Snivel pressed a button behind his ear and a holographic image appeared in the air projected from his third eye. It showed the alien fish creature they had just encountered.

"That's it," said Oscar.

"But what is it?" demanded Zana.

"That's a Grackle-Shaffler," announced the Snot-Bot.

"Grackle-Shaffler?" chorused Jack and Oscar

"Your dog can *talk*?" said Zana.

"Er... yes," said Jack. "He's built with alien technology."

"He's powered by snot," said Oscar.

Zana pulled a face. "Ugh," she said. "That's gross."

"Anyway," interrupted Jack, seeing the offended expression on Snivel's face. "Tell us about this Grackle-Shaffler thing, Snivel."

"Semi-intelligent life-form from a completely water-covered planet in the Amity System," explained Snivel. "Eats ten times its own body weight in smelly seaweed and jellyfish every day. Analysis of the waters around here suggests that it's been feasting ever since it arrived. Probably explains why it hasn't been looking for Bad

Bob as urgently as it should have been."

"But now I don't need to," said a peculiar electronic voice close by. They all looked down and saw that a beach buoy had joined them on the platform. It was the same one that Jack and Oscar had seen earlier on the beach. Only now it had grown a pair of mechanical legs and a pair of mechanical arms from its buoy-like body and was climbing on to the concrete base where they were gathered. Some kind of alien weapon was clasped in one metallic hand and it was pointed directly at them.

"What's that?" demanded Zana, clearly reaching the limit of her ability to cope with weirdness.

"CATS Suit," said Snivel helpfully.

"How is that a cat suit?" asked Oscar.

"Compact All Terrain Survival Suit," explained Snivel. "It's used by Grackle-Shafflers to operate out of the water."

"But that alien fish was huge," said Zana. "It couldn't fit in there."

"That's the compact bit," Snivel told her patiently. "It's dimensionally transcendental."

"Like Bad Bob's base," added Jack.

"Talking of which..." interrupted the Grackle-Shaffler from within its metallic CATS Suit. "I was hoping someone might show me the way and now you've arrived to do just that. So which one of these wind turbines is the prison holding my alien allies?"

Jack and Oscar exchanged a quick look. Should they play for time?

"Come on, humans, I don't have all day."

"We'd show you," Jack told him, "but you destroyed our boat."

105

"You need transport?" asked the alien.

Jack didn't like the sound of that. His plan, such as it was, depended on *not* having a means to leave the platform they were on.

"No problem," continued the alien. "I'll take you."

Jack closed his eyes for a moment. Why could *nothing* ever go according to plan?

Ruby was worried. Ever since her text message she had been waiting to hear from the boys, but there had been no contact. Her instincts were telling her that Jack and Oscar needed help, but what could she do? She didn't even know exactly where they were. She guessed that they had gone to Brilcombe to check out the shark story, but that hardly narrowed it down very much.

It was Brownie night, but on her way to the Pack meeting Ruby took the long route and found herself near Oscar and Jack's houses. There was no sign of life in the tree house so Ruby decided to take a closer look. For a girl as active as Ruby it didn't take much to climb over the garden fence and clamber up the tree to the shed which was the boys" base.

Ruby hoped that they had left some kind of message for her, but there was nothing. She looked around the workshop area carefully. No clues there. The only thing she *did* find was the remote control device they'd taken from Bad Bob's base. She could see that Jack had been working on it to make some kind of detector and she remembered getting a text from the boys when they had failed to make it work.

Ruby got her mobile out of her pocket and checked her messages. What exactly had Oscar said? She re-read the message quickly. So the scanner had prove to be useless because all it picked up were the signals from Snivel. Which meant that it was useless as an alien detector but perfect as a Snivel detector! And if she could find Snivel, then she'd find the boys too...

Ruby picked up the device and switched it on. Grinning, she set off to get her bike. It looked like she might not make the Brownies meeting after all.

CHAPTER EIGHT

'Straight ahead,' ordered Jack, clinging on for dear life.

He was riding a rubber shark, legs wrapped around its body, and hands clinging to its neck. Behind him, Oscar was holding on to his waist and Zana was at the back, holding on to Oscar in a similar fashion. It was like one of those bananas that get

dragged behind speedboats, only a shark instead of a banana. Meanwhile, Snivel was hanging around Jack's neck like a furry backpack. Inside the shark suit, squeezed into the space that they had thought suitable for a human head, was the CATS Suit buoy containing the Grackle-Shaffler. The alien was able to project his voice from

within the suit through the shark body, so they could still hear him.

"This is the third one," complained the alien.

"I'm sorry," replied Jack, "but until we get right up close, they all look the same. Anyway, you're the one going slowly."

"It's my shark suit," said

the alien. "And it wasn't designed to carry passengers."

"So what *was* it designed for?" asked Oscar.

"I thought it would attract less attention. People would think it was odd if a buoy moved around, and I certainly couldn't keep my true form. A giant fish with a lantern on its head would be a real talking point!"

"Right…" said Jack. "Whereas a shark off the coast of England is really inconspicuous."

"That was my reasoning, yes," said the alien, the irony clearly lost on it. "And it worked very well, until you lot came and fished my shark suit out of the water! Now, stop wasting time with questions and find me the base. I must send a message to my allies."

"We've got to do something," whispered Oscar in his ear.

Jack leaned back as best he could and nodded. "We're *going* to. Snivel, get ready. Oscar, tell Zana to jump to the right when I shout 'now'. We're going to try and turn the shark upside down."

Snivel coughed to get Jack's attention. "This is the one," he whispered urgently.

Jack looked up and could see that they were almost at the next turbine. Time for his daring plan.

"Now!" he shouted. Together he, Oscar and Zana pulled to the right, while keeping their legs firmly holding on to the shark's body. Like a canoe doing a three sixty, the shark twisted and spun. As soon as they hit the water, the humans relaxed their legs and swam away. As Jack had planned, the shark continued to turn, going belly-up and exposing the CATS Suit containing the

Grackle-Shaffler to the air. For a moment it lay there, stuck in the spherical hole in the base of the shark suit. Jack broke the surface and saw that Snivel was doggy-paddling back to the shark and diving beneath it. As

soon as the Snot-
Bot was under the
alien, Jack rolled
the shark suit to flip
it over, then called
out the command
words.

"Activate Snivel
Trap!"

Instantly Snivel
transformed into a
metallic box with
impenetrable sides
which snapped
shut, locking the

alien Grackle-Shaffler (CATS Suit and all) inside, leaving the shark suit empty.

Zana, Jack and Oscar swam to the body suit and used it as a float to get to the nearby turbine. Together they hefted the

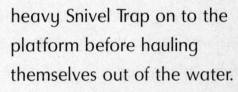

heavy Snivel Trap on to the platform before hauling themselves out of the water.

"I don't think I ever want to see the sea again," complained an exhausted Oscar.

"What just happened?" asked Zana, utterly confused.

"We just captured an alien with our transforming robot dog, of course," said Jack. "Try and keep up."

"But we're still stuck out here," pointed out Zana. "So no change there!"

An awkward silence descended on the group as the truth of Zana's words hit home.

Suddenly there was the sound of a small engine and a boat roared up alongside them. "Hi guys," said a familiar voice. "Do you need a lift?"

"Ruby!" cried Oscar and Jack in delight as they saw who was piloting the little boat. "What are you doing here? How did you find us?"

Ruby explained that she had used the tracker they had made to find out exactly where they were.

"And the boat?"

"Belongs to Brown Owl," confessed Ruby. "I think I might get kicked out of the Brownies when she finds out I've borrowed it." Ruby nodded in the direction of the Snivel Trap. "Looks like I've missed the fun bit."

Oscar shook his head violently. "Trust me, you didn't miss anything that was remotely fun."

Jack explained about the thirteenth turbine being Bad Bob's base.

"So how do we get inside?" wondered Ruby. "There's no door."

Jack reached out and took the scanner that he had made from Bad Bob's remote control. Stripping off the components he had added he soon had the original device in his hands. Pointing it at the turbine he pressed a combination of buttons and suddenly all of them were... somewhere else.

Jack opened his eyes. The teleport always made him a little dizzy and disorientated so

he was relieved to find himself inside the familiar corridors of the GUNGE base. It was, however, very different to the last time he had been here. It was dark and quiet and felt a bit unloved. A few groans alerted Jack to the fact that the others were also inside the base with him.

"Looks like Bad Bob isn't at home," whispered Oscar, joining him.

"Be careful," suggested Jack. "The four aliens we captured might still be out of their cells."

It was a reasonable suggestion, but a quick check of the cells proved otherwise. The four aliens they had captured on previous missions were all locked up, and all in a state of suspended animation. Jack used the remote control device to add the Grackle-Shaffler to the collection and to revert Snivel to his usual form.

"So can we use that to send this base back to the mainland?" wondered Ruby.

Jack shrugged. "I don't know. I doubt it. There must be some kind of main control room somewhere. Let's spread out and take a look."

The three children and Snivel were so busy with their search that they completely forgot about Zana. It helped that Zana had spent the whole time since they had teleported into the base with her eyes wide open and her mouth shut. She looked in a complete state of shock. Oscar had asked if they should look for a drink of water for her or something but Ruby had suggested that they should just leave her in peace to get her mind around what was happening.

They left her sitting with her back to one of the cell windows in the main corridor.

Moments after the children left her, Zana raised her head and smiled. At last! Here was the evidence she needed. Five aliens all safely behind strengthened safety glass. All she needed was proof. She pulled out her mobile phone and switched it on. Despite the soakings she had endured today, it was still working. There was no signal but that didn't matter. She didn't want to use it as a phone right now; all she was interested in was the camera function.

She held up the phone and lined up her first shot – the alien they had just captured. The Grackle-Shaffler. Hardly daring to breathe she steadied her hands and operated the control. FLASH! She allowed herself a grin. One down, four to go.

And then utter chaos erupted. Emergency red lights began to flash. An alarm sounded. A recorded computer voice began to speak.

"Unauthorised photographic recording device detected. Initiate Defence Protocol Three. Emergency occupant purge and relocation in ten seconds."

Elsewhere in the base Ruby and Snivel were listening to the same announcement.

"What does it mean?" asked Ruby.

"Nothing good!" replied Oscar.

In another part of the base Jack and Snivel were also reacting to the cacophony.

"There may be a manual override," said Snivel, "if I can find it in time."

But then there was a massive flash of white light and when it faded the four humans and Snivel found themselves back in the Brownie boat. The thirteenth turbine had completely disappeared.

"It's gone!" Ruby screamed. "We found it and now it's gone again!"

"And it's all your fault!" Jack pointed a finger at Zana.

"All I did was take a photograph!" she explained.

"Snivel!"

Snivel knew exactly what to do. He opened his third eye and directed the beam of energy at the phone in Zana's hand.

"Alien image removed," he announced after a moment.

"You can't do that. That was my proof. Without that my story sounds like the ramblings of a raving lunatic," she complained.

"In that case," suggested Ruby, "I'd keep it to yourself."

"But… but… I'm a journalist. I have to have *some* story from all this," said Zana, apparently on the verge of tears.

Jack took pity on her. He reached back in the boat and dragged the empty shark suit towards him.

"Here you are," he said kindly to Zana. "Your exclusive: 'Brilcombe shark a student prank!' All the evidence you need."

"But what student? Who should I say wore the suit?" Zana moaned.

Ruby and Oscar laughed. "Does it matter? An unidentified student is better than a jellyfish-eating alien inside a beach-buoy-shaped survival suit any day of the week!"